W9-BUE-830

Some other books by Mary Stolz

AND LOVE REPLIED
THE BEAUTIFUL FRIEND AND OTHER STORIES
BECAUSE OF MADELINE
BELLING THE TIGER
THE BULLY OF BARKHAM STREET
THE DAY AND THE WAY WE MET
A DOG ON BARKHAM STREET
FRÉDOU
GOOD-BY MY SHADOW
THE GREAT REBELLION
HOSPITAL ZONE
IN A MIRROR
MAXIMILIAN'S WORLD
THE NOONDAY FRIENDS
THE ORGANDY CUPCAKES
PIGEON FLIGHT
PRAY LOVE, REMEMBER
READY OR NOT
ROSEMARY
SAY SOMETHING
THE SEA GULLS WOKE ME
SECOND NATURE
SIRI THE CONQUISTADOR
SOME MERRY-GO-ROUND MUSIC
TO TELL YOUR LOVE
WAIT FOR ME, MICHAEL
A WONDERFUL, TERRIBLE TIME

The Dragons of the Queen

The Dragons of the Queen

by Mary Stolz

Pictures by Edward Frascino

HARPER & ROW, PUBLISHERS New York, Evanston, and London

 For information address Harper & Row, Publishers, Incorporated, 49 East 33rd Street, New York, N.Y. 10016. Published simultaneously in Canada by Fitzhenry & Whiteside Limited, Toronto.
Library of Congress Catalog Card Number: 69-14442

To Roslyn and Bill Targ

The Dragons of the Queen

The queen was not a real queen and the dragons were not real dragons. But to the people of the town, Dona Pascuala, who lived in a castle with dragons to guard her, was a descendant of kings. The castle was an old *hacienda,* and it was crumbling. When strangers asked what held it together, Dona Pascuala would answer proudly "Tradition, dignity, and vines."

Dona Pascuala was a hundred and two years old. She wore a crown on her black hair. Nobody knew whether it was a real crown or just a ring of glitter she had found somewhere sometime during her one hundred and two years. Still, she held her head high and the crown flashed when she moved. She looked a royal woman as she moved through the walks and gardens of her time-eaten castle with the seven dragons frothing at her heels.

The dragons were named Luis, Paco, Salvador, Esteban, Manuel, Velas, and Harald. Harald was from north of the border and his blood lines were not good. But he was loyal to the queen and could make more noise than all the other dragons together, so everyone accepted him as an oddity.

One evening, as on all evenings, the bells were ringing the sun down behind the far hills and all the birds of the desert were flying in to roost on the roofs and eaves and trees of the village square. This time a large automobile came down the hilly cobbled streets and parked in front of the *posada.*

"Posada," said the man at the wheel. He was a chauffeur.

The people in the back seat looked at each other. They were Mr. and Mrs. George Kenilworth from just outside Boise, Idaho. They did not speak Spanish, the language spoken in Mexico, which is where they were this evening in the dusk in their big car.

"*Posada,*" said the chauffeur again and translated for them: "Hotel."

"I know that by now," Mr. Kenilworth muttered crossly.

His wife said, "Really, George. I do not wish to spend the night in this dreary little town."

"It's too far to go on tonight. Having the car break down was very bad luck. We'll just have to make the best of it. Be brave, my dear."

"Very well," she said, looking brave. "Go and get us rooms," she said to the chauffeur.

"*Por favor,*" said Mr. Kenilworth. He had picked up a few words of Spanish, in spite of not trying. "*Por favor* means please," he said to his wife.

"George, how wonderful you are. First thing we know, we'll be speaking like natives."

They laughed together.

"Why learn Spanish?" George had often said during their trip. "The only person we ever get to talk to is our driver."

"And he does all the talking for us," his wife would add.

They were a lazy couple, but cheery enough if all

POSADA
TERESA

went smoothly—by which they meant if everything went their way.

Tonight everything was not to go their way.

The bells rang and the starlings sang and the woman covered her ears. "Isn't there some way to stop them?" she pleaded.

"Can't think of any," said Mr. Kenilworth. "However, my dear, I'll do what I can." He got out of the car.

He stood in the square and looked around.

There was a large rectangle of trees in a garden in the square, and the trees were bursting with blackbirds, all calling their evening song in harsh tones. Across the square, a great pink plaster church resounded with ringing, swinging bells, and from other parts of the town smaller churches pealed smaller songs.

The more he watched and listened, the more Mr. Kenilworth realized that he wasn't going to be able to do anything about any of it. But still he did not get back into the car. He looked about him at the flowers in the garden, pearly and purple and scarlet and gold. He looked at the populace lounging on benches, taking their ease in the setting sun. He watched the children going by, hand in hand, talking rapidly to one another.

"Spanish, of course," George muttered to himself. He felt put out that children could speak a language he could not. As they went past they looked at him and giggled. He got back into the car.

"You're right," he said to his wife. "It's a terrible town." After a moment he added, "Pretty though. Have to give it that."

His wife seemed surprised. She looked out of the window for the first time. She saw people lounging easily on benches in the park, and brilliant flowers springing in the garden, and the pink plaster church decorated like an anniversary cake. She saw the children going by, hand in hand.

Now that the birds were still, the bells silent, the town growing quiet in the deep rose evening, she was ready to say it was pretty. Sort of pretty. Since they had to spend the night here, there was little use in continuing to say how awful it was.

Anyway, they'd only spend one night.

The driver came out of the hotel.

"Ah, Paco," said the man eagerly. "I hope you got us good rooms? The very best?"

"I got you no rooms at all, *senor,*" said Paco, lifting his shoulders.

"What's this?" said Mrs. Kenilworth.

"There are no rooms, *senora.*"

"How can there be no rooms," George demanded,

"when we have to spend the night here? What do you mean—no rooms?"

"*Senor*, I mean their rooms are all filled, *ocupado*. There is nothing for you. *Nada*. Nothing."

"I think I'm going to faint," said the woman.

"Edith, be brave," said her husband. "Let me take care of this." He strode into the hotel.

Paco, the driver, peered into the car, curious to see if the woman had fainted. She had not. She was fanning her face with a perfumed handkerchief. She looked very, very annoyed.

Paco straightened and leaned against the fender, waiting for the *senor* to come out again, which he did, quickly, his face dark and furious.

"There aren't any rooms!" he said, as if it were the first any of them had heard of it.

"Where's another hotel, Paco?" said Mrs. Kenilworth.

"No other hotel, *senora*," Paco said brightly. "*Posada Santa Teresa*. That's it. *Ningun otro*."

"Well, what are we supposed to do?" George Kenilworth demanded. "I suppose we'll have to push on for the border."

"Oh, no, *senor*," said Paco. "Not at night. For one thing, I am tired. For two things, I am afraid of the dark. For three things—"

"All right, all right. But what do we do?"

TERESA

Paco pinched his chin thoughtfully. "I could myself sleep on a bench over there in the park. But I do not think—no, I do not think that would do for you and the *senora.*"

"I don't think that either," said George Kenilworth firmly. "Mrs. Kenilworth and I cannot sleep in the park on a bench. You'll have to come up with another idea."

Paco tugged gently at his earlobe. "You might maybe sleep in the castle."

Edith Kenilworth brightened. "Castle?"

"What castle?" said Mr. Kenilworth suspiciously.

"*Senor,*" said Paco, speaking slowly, in a tone of awe. "There is in this town a castle—a *hacienda* in truth, but still a castle—hundreds of years old, and a queen lives there. She has seven dragons to guard her, and she has one hundred and two years." He stopped.

"Well? Well?" said Mr. Kenilworth. "What has this to do with us? You mean Her Royal Highness takes roomers?"

"She sometimes is so kind as to put up wayfarers," Paco said guardedly.

"I'll bet. And what's the going rate for rooms in a castle when the only hotel is full up?" George Kenilworth's normally pleasant face was not so pleasant now. He was tired, hungry, and sure he was about to be taken. A castle! A queen! Dragons!

"No rates," said Paco, shaking his head. "The queen does not charge for her hospitality."

"Then what's the catch?"

"Catch, *senor*?"

George looked helplessly at his wife.

"What Mr. Kenilworth is asking," said Mrs. Kenilworth to Paco, "is—ah—why? Why is the queen so kind as to sometimes put up wayfarers for nothing?"

"Because she is so kind," said Paco, looking from one to the other of his exhausted charges, as if wondering if he had not used the correct words. "Kind," he repeated. "Only—"

"Ah-hah!" said George. "I knew it. Now it comes. Only what, Paco?"

"Only, *senor*—the queen has to like you. That is to say, no one is turned away from the castle if the hotel is full up, but you may not dine with Dona Pascuala, or talk with her, or even see her if she does not like you."

George Kenilworth took out a handkerchief and wiped the top of his head. "How will she know if she likes us if she doesn't see us?" he asked irritably.

"She has her ways," Paco said mysteriously.

"Peepholes in the castle stronghold," said Mrs. Kenilworth, who was beginning to look forward to the adventure.

"Just get us to the castle, Paco," said Mr. Kenilworth

wearily. "I don't care if she talks to us or dines with us or even looks at us—just so we get something to eat and a place to sleep."

"Dragons," Mrs. Kenilworth mused. "What do you think, George? Not gila monsters surely?"

"Probably some carved junk in the driveway," George grumbled. "The country's full of images and if they aren't plumed serpents, they're undoubtedly dragons. I wish we'd gone to Yellowstone."

Mrs. Kenilworth took his hand and patted it as the car wound slowly up the cobbled hill and into the desert along a rutted road that in the headlights scarcely looked a road at all—just a flattened place in a rocky landscape.

After what seemed a long time, Paco turned in between a pair of stone pillars that started up without seeming purpose, for there was no wall or fence or even driveway for them to mark. They were just there—like two stone trees in the desert—and beyond them the dark, harsh, flat land went on.

Just when Mr. Kenilworth had concluded that the two stone pillars were all that was left of the castle, Paco said heartily, "*Entrada!*"

"*Entrada* to what?" Mr. Kenilworth demanded. He sounded irritable but was in truth more hungry than angry and more tired than hungry. All I want, he thought, is to lie down.

"Why, the entrance," said Paco. "At any moment now we will be at the castle itself." He turned around. "May I say, with all respect, *senor y senora,* that when we arrive it is maybe more better for me to talk?" The car swerved and Mrs. Kenilworth squealed. "A thousand pardons," said Paco, giving his attention again to the road.

"Why can't we speak for ourselves?" Mr. Kenilworth asked. "I am accustomed to speaking for myself."

"Dona Pascuala," said Paco, dropping his voice as if he were already in her royal and ancient presence, "is a most waning lady of one hundred and two years. She is able to bear only the lowest, softest of sounds. It has something to do," Paco said apologetically, "with her ears."

"You mean I yell?" George Kenilworth said loudly. "I like that. What do you think of that, Edith? Now let me tell you, *Senor* Paco," he went on, his voice rising on each syllable, "I am not accustomed to—"

"George," said Mrs. Kenilworth. "George." She patted his hand again. "Let us do as Paco says. We are in his hands. For my part, I shall be happy to have him do the talking. Only to lie down—to rest—to have a roof over our heads—"

"*Aqui*!" said Paco. "Look, *senor, senora*! The castle!"

And there it was—a long, low, stone *hacienda* of many years and much neglect. In the moonlight it did resemble a castle, with its arches and stone traceries, its terraced

weed-rank lawns, its great size indistinct and uncertain in the shadows. Tall, plumy jacaranda trees grew everywhere and great-leaved rope-thick vines gripped the walls and thrust into the very foundations of the building. Somewhere in the night a fountain was splashing and a bittersweet scent lay lightly on the warm air.

In one far window a flickering light burned. Otherwise, the castle seemed asleep in the milky moonlight.

"She's retired. She's in bed," said Mrs. Kenilworth with a sob in her voice. "We'll have to go away!"

"No, no," said Paco. "It is all right, *senora.* I will rouse the queen."

"But—"

"She reads in her room, that is all. Dona Pascuala says that at one hundred and two years, sleep is only a brief messenger of the future and easily dismissed. Until, of course," he added sadly, "the day of no dismissal comes."

He got out of the car, went up to the great carved wooden doors, and pulled at an iron bell that sprang up and down, ringing and resounding, echoing in the night.

"I thought she didn't like loud noises," Mr. Kenilworth complained, putting his hands to his ears. As he spoke, a din burst forth that sent Mrs. Kenilworth into her husband's arms, where she cowered, her face against his chest.

"What is that?" she moaned.

"Sounds like a pack of mad dogs. Hungry mad dogs at that."

"*Los dragones*," said Paco proudly. "Here they come. The dragons of the queen!"

Down the colonnaded arcade came a rippling silver mass of what looked to Mrs. Kenilworth like huge caterpillars. She shrank closer against her husband's big chest and closed her eyes.

Mr. Kenilworth, of stouter stuff, faced the onrushing horde, which sorted itself into a pack of yelping pewter-colored Pekingese dogs. Behind them, halting every few yards to lift his head and bay earnestly, was a huge brown-and-white houndlike creature with no tail.

Behind them all, fluttering in black tatters, came a small figure leaning on a silver cane. She wore a crown of glitter on her black thick hair and carried a kerosene lantern that swung as she walked, throwing shadows wildly to one side and then the other.

"Oh, my gosh," said Mr. Kenilworth. "Here comes Her Highness."

Mrs. Kenilworth peered fearfully down the arcade.

"Well, I never—" she gasped. "I never—"

Paco, as the queen approached, made a low bow.

"*Buenas noches, Dona Pascuala*," he said in a reverent voice. "*Como esta*?"

"*Muy bien, gracias, Paco. Y usted*?" Her voice was

strong and vibrant, and it lifted above the clamor of the dragons.

"*Muy bien, senora, gracias.* Here we have *Senor y Senora* Kenilworth from the United States of America. The *posada,* alas, is unable to accommodate them. They are tired and in need of food."

"Ah, a thousand pities," said Dona Pascuala.

"She has a voice like an oboe," said Mr. Kenilworth. "I expected a flute."

He spoke in a whisper, but Dona Pascuala apparently had nothing wrong with her hearing. She smiled as if pleased.

The Pekingeses yelped, the hound dog bayed, and starlings, made restless by the invasion, began to scream.

"What was that about not liking loud noises?" Mr. Kenilworth muttered to Paco.

Paco shrugged and then said cheerfully, "I see, *senor*, that even at one hundred and two years one is able to change. A wonderful prospect, is it not?"

"What're the prospects for a meal and a night's lodging?" said George, still in a voice meant to be obscured by the frenzied dragons and starlings.

"They are excellent," said Dona Pascuala. "Come, Mr. and Mrs. Kenilworth. I will show you to your room, and then we shall all meet in the *sala* for food and conversation."

"Oh, but we wouldn't dream of putting you to any trouble—that is, of keeping you up—that is—"

Bed! George Kenilworth was thinking. We have to get to bed!

"A pleasure. An honor," said Dona Pascuala. "I sleep but little and relish any opportunity for the exchange of views. Come."

Mr. and Mrs. Kenilworth did not look at each other.

The queen led her entourage down the colonnaded arcade, along a narrow hallway lined with pictures they could not see, across a great shadowy tiled patio where the fountain was splashing in a stone basin, through an entrance at the other side, up a broad flight of stairs, down a wide hallway.

Paco, with the bags, followed Mr. and Mrs. Kenilworth. Behind him came the dragons, quiet now except for the clatter of their toenails on slate and tile. The lantern threw their silhouettes, and those of the small tattered queen, the two big North Americans, and lively Paco, up and down and sideways on walls and floors.

"Here we are," said Dona Pascuala, throwing open a door just as Mrs. Kenilworth began to think she and her husband had gotten into a dream of endless walking by lantern light in Mexico—or maybe in Eternity.

The room into which they stepped was vast in feeling, but the lantern light did not penetrate its reaches.

"Paco," said Dona Pascuala imperiously, "light the candelabra and then await our guests in the hall to show them down. I shall leave you now," she said to Mr. and Mrs. Kenilworth, "to see that Lola prepares dinner. You must be very hungry."

"Yes, but Your Highness, at this hour—dinner—that is to say—just a snack—"

The queen was gone.

Paco lighted the candles and glided out, closing the door behind him soundlessly. Mr. and Mrs. Kenilworth now looked at each other.

"Is it a dream?" said Mrs. Kenilworth at last. "George, do tell me we're back at home and about to wake up at any moment."

He shook his head. "We're awake," he said, then added, "barely. You and I, my dear, are in a Mexican castle, being entertained by royalty." He yawned and said, "Royalty that is apparently willing to stay up all night."

"I can't," said Mrs. Kenilworth.

"We must. Anyway, Edith," he said, and seemed all at once to shed his fatigue, "what an experience, eh? Nothing like this ever happened to us before. Nothing—magical like this—mysterious."

Indeed, in all their years nothing like this had ever happened to them before. Looked at in a certain way, it might be said that nothing had ever happened to them at all.

They had been born and had grown up in a little town just outside Boise. They'd married and raised children, and their children had married and moved away. Still Mr. and Mrs. George Kenilworth never left the outskirts of their home town.

Then on a day a couple of months earlier, Mr. Kenilworth had announced at dinner that they were going to take a trip.

"A trip?" Mrs. Kenilworth had said somewhat fearfully. "A trip where? And why, George?"

"Why? Because we've never been anyplace, that's why," George had said firmly. He didn't seem as certain when it came to the question of where. "Where would you like to go?"

"The—the Grand Canyon, maybe?"

"Snowed in this time of year."

"We could wait."

"No, no," George had said loudly. "Now is when I got this idea, and now is when we should do it. Who knows, if we wait, we might never go at all."

This was rather what Mrs. Kenilworth had in mind, but she said to herself that if this was what George wanted, it was what he should have.

"To—to—to Europe, maybe?" she'd said and had been

relieved when George shook his head.

"That's too far away." He'd sounded alarmed. "Europe. My gosh. Hey, I've got it! We'll go to Mexico. That's the ticket. I mean, after all, it's attached to our own country. We wouldn't have to go across the ocean or anything. Mexico," he repeated. "Just the thing."

But still they'd been reluctant to start off on such an adventure—just the two of them—until George read about how one could go to Mexico City and hire a driver who would take car and passengers anywhere they wished to go at any pace. You didn't need to know a word of Spanish, for the driver would do all the talking. George, who was not a good driver in Idaho, was confident he'd be a terrible driver south of the border, and neither of them had any Spanish. But this plan solved all their problems.

And so for over a month they had been touring in the capable hands of Paco, who would shortly deposit them in San Antonio, Texas, where he was to pick up another couple and drive them back down to Mexico City. The Kenilworths had seen the ancient pyramids and the jungles of Yucatan, the silversmiths of Taxco, the beaches at Acapulco, and a monastery at Yanhuitlan. They felt indeed that they had seen Mexico roundly and well, but they planned to come back one day for the things and places they'd missed.

But who ever would have expected this? Until this

night there had never been any trouble about room reservations. For that matter they had reservations for the night—only not in this town. Today for the first time something had gone wrong with the car—something severe that even Paco had been unequal to. For hours the Kenilworths had waited by the roadside while Paco trudged off to a garage they'd passed an hour before breaking down, and then for hours they'd waited while the mechanic Paco brought back with him had labored to get their engine working. He'd been good at his job, and the engine was running smoothly again. But now Mr. and Mrs. Kenilworth were a long way from their room reservations here in a castle with an old queen and her dragons.

Mrs. Kenilworth moved cautiously about the room. "This place is tremendous, George." She looked at the great bed canopied with worn velvet, at the huge dark wardrobe, at one carven chair, and the single table. "Can she really be a queen?"

"The last queen of Mexico was Carlota. Actually she was an empress. Probably the villagers just call Dona Pascuala a queen for a courtesy title, or something. Because she's so old maybe. Maybe she's awfully rich."

"She can't be rich. This place is falling apart."

"Maybe she's got royal blood in her veins. That's a possibility. Lots of Mexicans are descended from Spanish aristocracy."

"Just think of it," said Mrs. Kenilworth. Then so as not to sound too impressed, she added, "But why do they call those dogs dragons?"

George lifted his shoulders. "Pekes sort of look like dragons, don't they? With those squashed faces and fringy curled tails? And they seem to guard the place all right. Funny color, aren't they? Like silver. Seven silver dragons and a queen a hundred and two years old with a crown on her head. Who'd ever believe it?"

"Six silver dragons. That other one's a mutt. How do you suppose he got into the queen's guard?"

"Hey, look," said George. "Here's a bathroom. Bigger than our rumpus room I think." He turned on a faucet. A spider fell out and walked down the marble tub. George laughed and looked around, holding one of the candles up. "Edith, there's grass growing in this bathroom. It's coming up between the tiles."

"There's a pitcher and basin in here," she called. "And a thermos of ice water. And, George, the bed linen must be fifty years old. It's the most beautiful I've ever seen."

"I'm beginning to think," he said, "that maybe that breakdown was the luckiest part of our trip. I mean, look at us. Look at all this." He stepped out on the balcony,

first testing to be sure it wouldn't come away from the house. "Look, Edith."

The balcony faced the desert, where yucca plants gleamed like fans in the moonlight. Below them the fountain tossed and fell with a musical sound in its great stone bowl, and far off a coyote wailed and was answered by another coyote and yet another. In the dark and densely foliated gardens, iguanas clacked. "They sound like someone nailing up copper gutters," George said. He said it every time they heard the iguanas, and Mrs. Kenilworth always agreed because it was what they sounded like. An owl flew past, silhouetted for a soft swift moment against the moon.

Mr. and Mrs. Kenilworth, standing hand in hand on the balcony, sighed and marveled that they should be here.

"She must like us," George said at length. "Paco says she only converses with people that she takes to."

"He said she didn't like noise too," Mrs. Kenilworth pointed out. "In my opinion, she's probably lonely up here in the wilderness and willing to talk to anyone. It stands to reason, at one hundred and two she doesn't get around much anymore. I do hope," she added, her eyes on the huge comfortable-looking bed with its fragrant fresh old linen, "that she doesn't want to talk all night."

"We can always sleep," George said briskly. "When will we get to talk with a queen again?"

Paco knocked softly at the door. "*Senor, senora—la comida esta servida.*"

George and Edith followed him back down the wide hallway and the great staircase, across the patio, through another arcade, and into a great *sala.*

At the far side a little fire burned in a vast hearth, before which the dragons lay on a frayed and glowing ruby rug. There were candles on the mantel and on a table set for dinner. There were four high-backed, carved, massive chairs covered with dark red velvet and tarnished fringe. In one of these sat Dona Pascuala, looking small, upright, and majestic. There was no other furniture at all in the great room, but above the mantel was an oil painting of a beautiful young woman wearing a white *mantilla* and sitting before this very hearth in the very chair now occupied by Dona Pascuala. Six silver Pekingeses lay on what appeared to be the same ruby rug.

Edith and George Kenilworth stood still, looking from the picture on the wall to Dona Pascuala.

She smiled. "It is I. Painted eighty years ago. Was I not beautiful?"

"Very beautiful, Your Highness," said George softly. "Like a flower."

"No titles, please. Dona Pascuala I am called. Paco, Lola may serve us, *por favor.*"

The food was hot and spicy and delicious. After their

fast of nearly a day, George and Edith did not restrain their appreciation, but Dona Pascuala took only a little red wine. She turned and turned the stem of her glass and regarded them peacefully.

"Well, but Your Highness—I mean Dona Pascuala," George said at length. "How did you come to be a queen? I mean, what's back of it all?" Edith's foot nudged his, and he said hastily, "Excuse me for being nosy, *senora.* It's just—well, I can't help being curious."

"The town calls me a queen," said Dona Pascuala, lifting her frail shoulders in a gesture of acceptance. "Some are and some are not queens. Who is to say or be sure? I can say that my family tree, which goes back to the twelfth century, has thirteen crowns on it. Thirteen crowns," she repeated with dreamy pride, then grew silent.

They saw that the mystery of her queenship was to remain a mystery, and George decided it was just as well. He said many times after that night that some things in life ought to be mysterious and remain mysterious.

Dona Pascuala, however, was glad to talk of anything else. She told them about the painting and how the painter had posed her here so many years ago with the remote ancestors of Luis, Paco, Salvador, Esteban, Manuel, Velas, and Harald.

"Harald?" said Mrs. Kenilworth. "Surely not."

"Ah. Ah, yes." Dona Pascuala smiled. "I keep forgetting that he is not descended from silver dragons, as he forgets it himself, and that he is not, alas, represented in the portrait."

"Who is he descended from?" George asked, looking at tailless Harald, who stared pensively back.

"*Quien sabe*? Who knows? He came to the *hacienda* one day, starving and faint. Someone had dropped him from a passing car no doubt," she said sternly. "Some unspeakable type who didn't want him anymore and took this means of disposal. I fed him, and he attached himself to my guard. He has been most stalwart. In the beginning, I confess, I thought to give him away. He spoils the symmetry, you know." She regarded her small glistening cohorts with their flat, idol faces, and then looked at Harald, looming among them like an old stump starting out of the sea. "But no one would take him. He eats too much, and his voice is too deep. And he wouldn't leave me anyway," she said confidently.

"How come you called him Harald?" George asked.

"He was named for a guest of the time. And it is such a northern-sounding name, is it not? Harald. It fairly breathes chill climes."

"But Harald clearly considers himself a Mexican," said Edith.

At this repetition of his name, Harald leaped to his feet

and began to howl. Dona Pascuala implored him to be silent. Paco rushed into the room and begged him to desist. But Harald continued to call out that someone had named him and him alone, and he wanted to know the reason why.

"*Silencio*! *Silencio*!" cried Dona Pascuala. "*Silencio, Harald amigo*!"

But Harald kept on howling.

"Down boy!" said George Kenilworth without thinking.

Harald, in midhowl, grew still and sat.

"I'm not sure how Mexican he feels," said Dona Pascuala. "In all these years he has never learned a word of Spanish. And I never remember, in my frenzy to silence him at these times, how to say 'Down Boy.' "

At this Harald looked surprised, then flattened himself on the rug, nose on his paws. The Pekes sat in a circle around him, silent and watchful.

Mr. and Mrs. Kenilworth, their fatigue quite gone, sat with Dona Pascuala and listened to her oboelike voice as she told of past splendors in the *hacienda*. What balls and parties, what weddings and funerals, what christenings there had been. What music and dancing, what weeping and laughter, what joy and what loss. Her words wove a century of love and revolution and challenge and change.

"And now," she said at length, "here I am, quite alone, save for Lola and my seven faithful guardians."

"There is the town," George said. "They—the people of the town—revere you."

"Of course," said Dona Pascuala gracefully. "There is the town which I love. Upon which I depend, you understand. But the town is down there, and I am up here, alone on the hill. That is why it is good, now and then, that the *posada* fills up and I have the privilege of entertaining a wayfarer or two at my table, of exchanging views about the world."

Although in truth there had been no real exchange and Dona Pascuala had spoken only of a world now past, Mr. and Mrs. Kenilworth nodded agreement. Perhaps they had given Dona Pascuala something—their rapt attention, their high regard, their inexpressible astonishment at being here. But they were only two among the many wayfarers who had found and would find themselves enmeshed in fascination within her castle walls. For them she would remain forever unique—a glittering puzzle in their forthright, everyday lives.

In parting from her, Mr. Kenilworth bowed deeply, almost with the grace of Paco, and Mrs. Kenilworth very nearly curtsied.

"*Buenas noches, amigos,*" said Dona Pascuala, then laughed. "*Buenos dias*, I should say."

Indeed, the air stirring the long faded damask draperies was touched with morning freshness, and the sky outside the French doors was pale.

When Mr. and Mrs. Kenilworth got to their room, the candles that had been tall were guttering, sending up streamers of scented smoke before flickering out. Wordlessly the two travelers prepared for bed, thinking that nothing they could dream would be as strange as what they had just experienced.

They woke in the afternoon to the sound of a bell.

"George," said Edith, poking him. "George, what's that?"

"Church bell," he mumbled.

"I know. But are they—isn't it tolling?"

"Sure enough," said George, sitting up. "Somebody

died." He went to the window. "Edith," he called. "Edith, come here. Look there."

Winding slowly down the hill on a cart drawn by an old ivory-yellow horse was a small coffin. Behind the cart walked Paco, Lola, and the seven dragons. As the cortege progressed, people came out of their houses and followed it. They tossed flowers on the cart as it rattled down the road toward town.

"Can it be—it must be," Edith Kenilworth whispered. "It's Dona Pascuala. She has died since we saw her."

"Must be," George said softly. He sighed.

"How sad," said Mrs. Kenilworth.

"Oh, no. No, Edith. Remember what she said? That to someone who has one hundred and two years, death is no stranger. Death is a father arriving to take his child home from the party."

They recalled how she'd laughed. "My father comes rather late than soon, does he not? But he will come," she'd concluded peacefully. "Yes, he will come. And the party *has* been splendid."

"I wonder why no one woke us," George said.

"Because we aren't part of things here," said his wife. "They never thought of us."

"Not even Paco."

"No, not even Paco. He was so proud of Dona Pascuala, wasn't he?"

"Well, let's get dressed, Edith. Let's hurry to join the procession and do her honor." He looked from the balcony across the desert where many cactus flowers were blooming. The sun was gentle, the sky azure and untroubled.

"She has a good day for her journey, the little queen," said Mr. Kenilworth.

In the square the cart pulled up before the pink plaster church, and townsmen carried the coffin into the dark cool nave, resting it on a bier before the altar. Then, in a slow line, the people of the village filed past Dona Pascuala to bid her *adios.*

Out in the sun again, George and Edith Kenilworth found Paco on a bench.

"What happens now, Paco?" said Mr. Kenilworth.

The slender shoulders lifted and fell. "Now *senor?* Now no town in all Mexico has a queen."

"What will happen to the castle?" asked Edith.

"Ah, *que cosa,* the castle! Well, *senora,* the castle will now fall apart. Don Jorge, *el doctor,* will get the portrait of Dona Pascuala. Don Fernando, the *licenciado*—lawyer—will take what furniture there is since it all belongs to him anyway—"

"To the lawyer?" said George Kenilworth. "Not to Dona Pascuala?"

"*Senor*, many, many, many years ago, Dona Pascuala

came to the end of her last *peso*. Her father squandered an untellable fortune—all the riches his ancestors had left him—in one lifetime, and he left his daughter with nothing. *Nada*. Not a *peso*. So Don Fernando—this Don Fernando's grandfather, you understand—took over the *hacienda* and let Dona Pascuala stay there and provided for her needs, which she was most graceful to accept. And his son did the same, and his son the same, and we sometimes thought that his son would do the same. Indeed, I feel we had all come to think that Dona Pascuala would, in truth, and in defiance of nature, live forever. And now she is gone," he said mournfully.

"What happens to the dragons?"

Paco straightened and looked more cheerful. "Ah, *los dragones*. Long ago Dona Pascuala made disposition of her dragons for when she should be gathered to her fathers and they left behind. Don Fernando takes two, Don Jorge two, Don Luis one, and I, myself, am to have my namesake Paco. He will ride beside me in my big car and keep me company when I am alone."

"Do you think perhaps some of your passengers will object?" said Mr. Kenilworth. "Not everybody likes dogs, you know, Paco."

"*Senor*—if they object, I will get different passengers. Besides, who could be anything but proud to ride in the company of such a shining object, descended from nobility? Now, if it were that Harald—" He turned out his hands and lifted his eyes.

"But then, what will happen to Harald?" cried Mrs. Kenilworth.

"*Senora*, this is a sad cruel world we live in. It grieves me to say that—well, that no one knows what will happen to Harald. Even Don Fernando cannot think what disposition to make of him, and Dona Pascuala made her wishes clear before the arrival of Harald. How sad that she never got around to arranging for his future."

"Then what will his future be?" Mr. Kenilworth demanded.

"*Quien sabe*? He lived by his wits before the queen took him into her guard. No doubt he can live by his wits again."

"You mean you'll just turn him out? The way the people did who abandoned him in the first place?"

"*Senor*," said Paco patiently, "this is a poor town. Harald is too big. He's too noisy. He eats too much. Besides, he does not understand Spanish."

Indeed, in some way of his own, Harald seemed already to have sensed his loss of place. Inside the church the six silver Pekingeses sat still and sturdy around the queen's bier. But Harald was out in the square, wandering from place to place, looking from face to face. At length, he sat down, lifted his head, and began to howl.

"*Silencio*!" cried several of the villagers. "*Estese quieto*!"

Harald's melancholy voice filled the square, set the starlings shrieking and the children laughing. His loud and wavering lament mingled with the tolling of the bells.

"*Silencio*! *Silencio*!"

But Harald kept on wailing.

"Down boy!" said George Kenilworth.

Harald grew still. He turned and looked at the church, then walked slowly, head down, to sit between Mr. and Mrs. Kenilworth. He did not seem especially hopeful—just uncertain of what else to do.

George and Edith Kenilworth studied the big boney brown-and-white dog. They looked at each other and then at Paco, who stared up at the spire of the pink plaster church.

"Well," said George Kenilworth. "Well. How do you like that?"

Mrs. Kenilworth sighed. "I guess we've been left a bequest by the queen."

"I guess we have at that."

Paco regarded his two passengers proudly. He wondered if they knew how they had changed since meeting the queen. Mrs. Kenilworth didn't order him around now. Mr. Kenilworth didn't look as if people spoke Spanish only to annoy him. They did not appear to feel that everything was going well only as long as it went their way. Don Fernando had often told him that all her life long the queen had been able to touch people as if with a wand, and here, on her very last night, she had woven her magic for Harald's sake. And, yes, for the sake of the North Americans too.

How happy she must be, Paco went on to himself, looking up at the sky where Dona Pascuala must surely be looking down on her town.

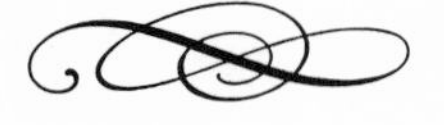

When the Kenilworths got home to the town outside Boise, they never told even their best friends that their homely, sweet-tempered, loud-voiced, rather gluttonous new pet had come right out of a royal guard of honor.

"For one thing," George pointed out to his wife, "no one would believe us. For two things, we'd be laughed at. For three things—"

"For three things," Mrs. Kenilworth would go on, "we had something magical and mysterious happen to us, and Harald is part of that mystery and magic. I don't think people should talk about magical and mysterious happenings, except to each other."

They would sit for a while, remembering the darkened castle with its vines and jacaranda trees and the iguanas clacking in the darkness. They would recall that small figure in fluttering black tatters, coming toward them in the lantern light—crown aglitter—with the seven dragons frothing at her heels.

Harald, between them, would sigh in his sleep, turning his boney head from side to side, as if he too recalled other, grander times, when he had been a dragon and served a queen.

When he began to snort and whimper and mumble through his dreams, Mr. Kenilworth would say "*Silencio, Harald! Silencio!*"

Harald, who had finally learned a word of Spanish, would grow still—happy to hear in this foreign land the accent of the town he dreamed of.

Format by Ruth Bornschlegel
Set in Linotype Caledonia
Composed by American Book–Stratford Press, Inc.
Printed by Halliday Lithograph Corp.
Bound by Publishers Book Bindery
HARPER & ROW, PUBLISHERS, INCORPORATED